MY DAD IS A BEAR

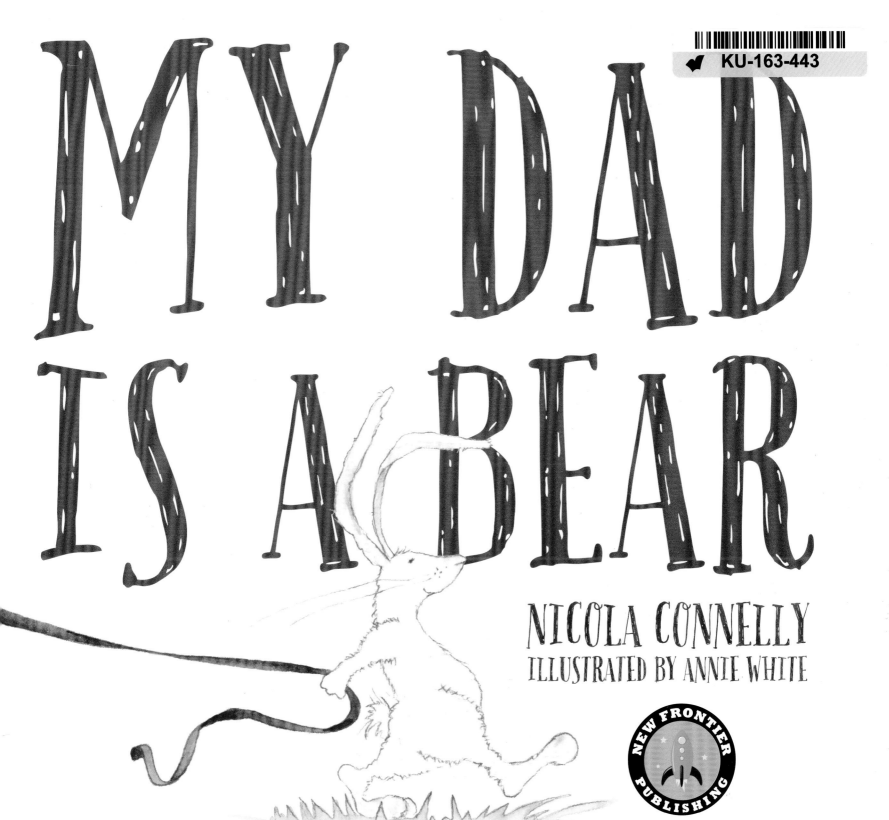

NICOLA CONNELLY

ILLUSTRATED BY ANNIE WHITE

NEW FRONTIER PUBLISHING

My dad is a bear.

MY DAD IS A BEAR

For my Dad, the cuddliest bear I know. NC

To the fathers in my family:
Graham, Ian, Andy and Jack. AW

He is tall and round like a bear.

He is soft and furry like a bear.

He climbs and gathers
like a bear.

He even has big paws like a bear!

He scratches his back like a bear.

He sure can growl like a bear.

He goes fishing like a bear.

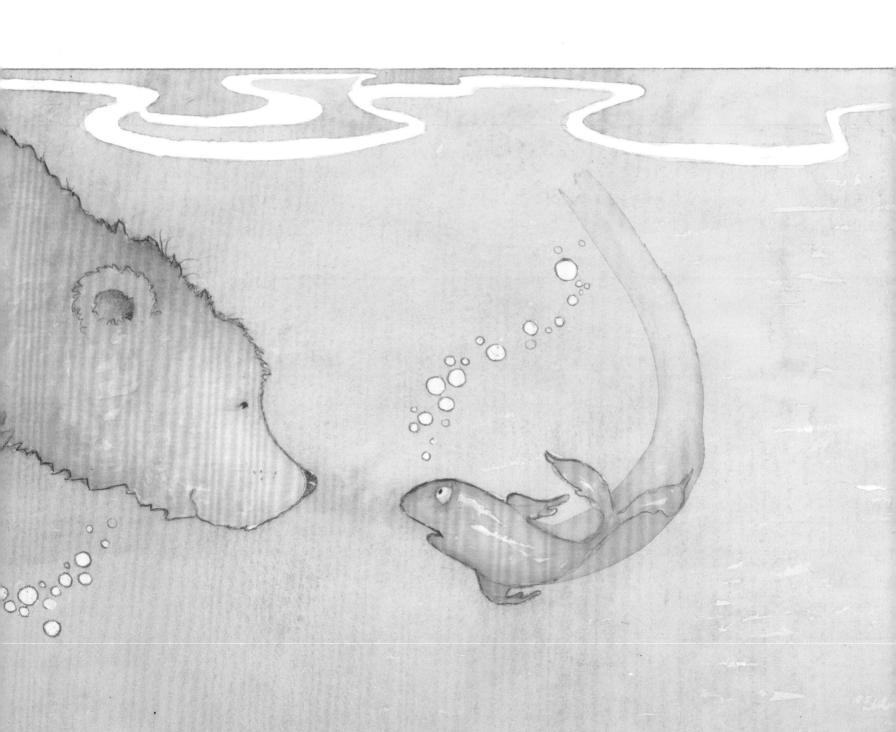

He even sleeps like a bear!

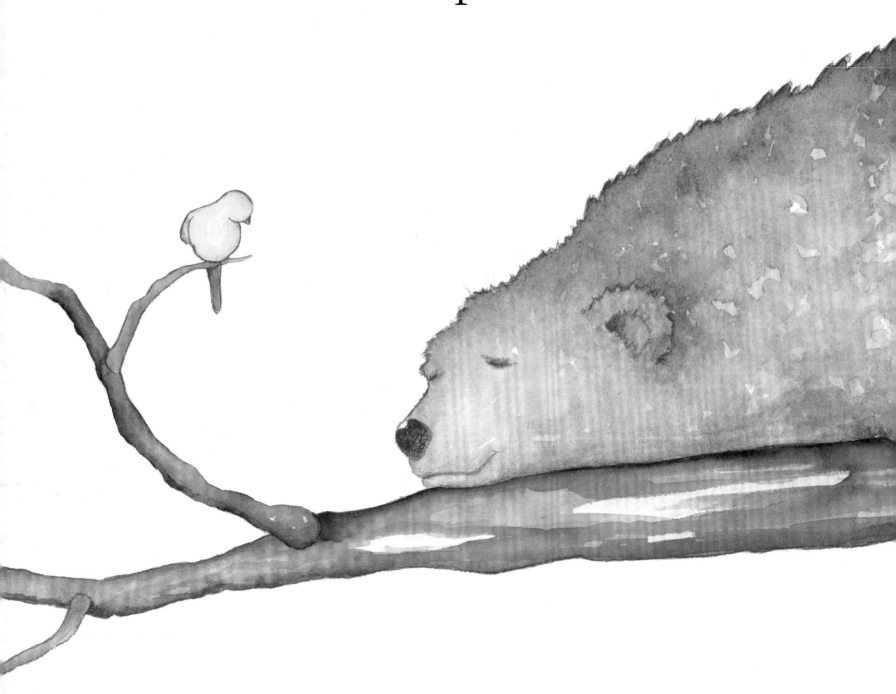

So one day I asked, 'Dad, are you *really* a bear?'

'Well, of course I am Charlie, and do you know what bears do best?'

'No.' I said.

'Give bear hugs!'

First published in the UK in 2017
by New Frontier Publishing Pty Ltd
93 Harbord Street, London SW6 6PN
www.newfrontierpublishing.co.uk

ISBN: 978-0-9956255-8-7 (PB)

Text copyright © Nicola Connelly 2014
Illustrations copyright © Annie White 2014

A CIP catalogue record for this book is
available from the British Library.

Designed by Celeste Hulme

Printed in China
10 9 8 7 6 5 4 3 2 1